HE OWNS ME

Dark Hucow BDSM

Leandra Camilli

ISBN: 9798847966153
Imprint: Independently published

1st edition

Cover design by: Leandra Camilli

CONTENTS

Title Page

Copyright

Chapter 1   1

Chapter 2   5

Chapter 3   8

Chapter 4   11

Chapter 5   14

Chapter 6   17

Epilogue   20

Teaser: I'm his Property   23

Similar Books   27

About the Author   29

CHAPTER 1

"Wait, you are not telling me that you are a virgin, right?" My friend asked me. He was with me and I was in his house. We were here having a typical party that happened every time we were together. I had just come here from work. I was traveling abroad and I decided to come here so that we could catch up on some things. There were so many things that were happening in his life, after all.

And one was that he was with a certain auction club. I didn't know what it was about exactly, but he was so jubilant about it when he was talking with me about everything on the phone. He even told me that he was now married, though I couldn't see his wife anywhere.

There were signs in his house that he was already married, but I didn't even see a portrait of them in the house. I wondered what was up with that. But I wasn't really worried about it. What I was concerned about was the fact that he just asked me if I was a virgin or not, and me being me, how was I going to not answer that question, especially when he was being so nice to me, giving me everything?

His eyes were… Intense, to say the least. He had his attention fully focused on me and I didn't know how to react to that. That was why I was feeling so uncomfortable, shifting my weight all the time while I was sitting on the couch.

He chuckled. "Is it really because you are so skinny and your breasts are so small?" He asked me, making my cheeks blush deep red. I never thought that he was going to ask me that question and was going to do it so bluntly.

It was true, I thought, looking down at my body. I tried my best, tried to buy the best clothes possible, but the truth was that not even the best clothes and not even the best treatments – that weren't too invasive – could do much to change my body. I always looked at those photos of those women on the Internet and I always imagined how lucky they were to have such curvy bodies.

But that was all in the past. At least, that was what I was telling myself anyway.

"Yeah, I still am. I really should not be saying anything about that to you right now, though," I said, hoping that he was going to change the subject, but given the way that he was staring at me, it was obvious that he wasn't going to drop it so soon.

"If it bothers you so much, there is something that we could do about it."

"If you are thinking that I'm going to have sex with you, then you are delusional. I'm not going to do that. You are a friend of mine, I think you're hot, but that's where it all ends. I don't want to help you cheat on your wife, who you just recently married."

He sighed, shaking his head. "I was actually thinking about something else. There is this auction club that I go to often, and I think that they are looking for people like you. They say that they have a treatment that is going to change your body forever, and you only have to sign their contract so that they can sell you to someone who might be interested in you. By signing the contract, you will become that person's property and you will have to do everything they want you to do."

I widened my eyes immediately, not believing that I was going to become someone's property. The first thought that popped up into my mind was that I shouldn't do it at all, but then I looked down at my body and I reminded myself how much I hated it, and nothing was going to change that.

"You really don't want to do it?" Marcos asked, winking.

Oh, gosh. The winking. How was I going to say no to something like that? I thought, already feeling some wetness in my pussy. The truth was that the thought of becoming someone's property was tempting. Not to mention the fact that I would be in an auction club, too.

Fuck. Just the thought of all that happening was enough to make me decide on it right away.

"Alright, I guess that this is really happening," I said and he put down the glass that he was holding in his hand. Then, he stood up, his hands taking off his belt. Wait, what the fuck? I asked myself, realizing that this was indeed happening.

"But there's something that you should do for me first. Otherwise, I won't be telling anyone in the auction club about this," he informed, making me drop my jaw. What the fuck was going on with him? Was Marcos really so tempted to cheat on his wife with me? And here I thought that he was happily married to her.

Or maybe he'd always been an asshole and only now was I noticing that. Either way, I didn't like it, even though the thought of sucking him off made me water my mouth.

"Your wife…"

"Forget her. She isn't here. I want you," he said, lowering his pants and showing, for the delight of my eyes, his big, monstrous cock. I couldn't help but look at it and wonder how it was so big.

I also put the glass I was holding back on the coffee table, wrapping my lips around his big, massive, meaty manhood. If this was happening and it really was, then there was no point in pretending that I didn't want it.

So, I went down on his dick, swirling my tongue around it. He put his hand on the back of my head, grabbed a handful of my hair, and then dictated the pace, not letting the fact that this was the first time I was giving head – and thus, was deeply inexperienced – change his thoughts about this. If anything, he was enjoying this a lot more than he should.

Marcos came in my mouth in record time, looking slightly disappointed in himself.

"Sorry. I suppose that I should have held on for a little while longer, but even though you are still a virgin, I can't deny that you are hot and I've always thought about this moment, wondering how I was going to fuck your mouth. It was breathtaking, dear."

And with that said, I knew that my life, from now on, was going to be so different from what it could be.

CHAPTER 2

So, it happened and here I was, in front of his house. This was Geoffrey's house. That was his name and I just couldn't stop thinking about it. I couldn't stop thinking about what he looked like, too, and in person. I was certain that he was someone powerful, someone with a lot of influence in so many spheres in this city. His house was big too, I thought.

After all, I was in front of the door and, before coming here, I had the chance to take a look at the place from afar. It was so big. So pretty, so modern looking, and the area around it was dotted with all kinds of gardens, trees, and other entertainment or decoration options. The truth was that, after coming here, I could imagine myself living in this place for the rest of my life.

Geoffrey had already made the purchase. I thought that the sales associate was going to come here with me to show the place around to me and what I should expect from this little arrangement with Geoffrey, but he said that it wasn't going to be needed.

The funny thing about that was that he was uncomfortable when saying that to me, so I wondered if there was something else behind his explanation that he didn't want to share with me.

The door opened suddenly and I found myself inside the house. I started to explore it, wondering where my owner was. That was the only term that could properly describe him. He was my owner, and I just wanted to know where he was so that we could finally start this.

When Marcos fucked my mouth with his cock, he didn't go all the way and take my virginity, so right now I was wondering when I was going to find my owner so that he could finally do his duty.

But it was like someone was playing a trick on me. I started to explore every room in his house, hoping that I was going to catch sight of him, but the more I walked and the more I explored this place, the more I couldn't find anything.

My eyes caught sight of a door by my side. There were signs on it that showed it was used often and that nobody was careful with it when using it. I wondered why that was. It was the only door in the house that I had not opened yet. When exploring the place, I'd also noticed that there were signs, clothes, and some other things that showed me that someone else lived here with Geoffrey. Someone that he cared about…

I was already feeling jealous. If he already had someone else, then why the hell did he buy me? I asked myself, shaking my head in disappointment. No point in dwelling on that.

I opened the door and started to descend the steps that led to the basement.

It was dark and I felt shivers running down my spine, especially when I found someone by one of the walls, chained to it. Who that person was, I didn't know, but it was obvious that she was going through something terrible. It had to be someone that Geoffrey knew. He was keeping her here in captivity and was probably doing some pretty nasty BDSM stuff to her.

I knew that because the moment when she heard me coming, she lifted her head. Her eyes were red and her cheeks had cuts on them. She smiled defiantly, chuckling.

"So, you are his new plaything, aren't you?" She asked. She wasn't just looking hurt, but she was also naked, I noticed now that my eyes were better adjusted to the darkness.

The interesting thing about this was that she couldn't be someone like me – a hucow. She was just a normal person. I noticed that thanks to her lack of curves. She wasn't as curvy as I was.

"New plaything?" I asked when I heard someone coming down

the stairs. I turned around and I found him. I knew that it was him thanks to his photo on the application website. Geoffrey.

He was still with his office suit on as if he had just come from a business meeting. His eyes were serene, but his smile was devilish. I felt shivers running down my spine again. Just looking at him, I felt utterly submissive.

"It's you, isn't it? Your name is Sharon. You are cute," he said and, for a moment, I didn't know what to say. But I supposed that I had to do the nice thing and say something he wanted to hear.

"Yeah, it's me. I'm Sharon. You bought me, Master."

He stepped until he was right in front of me and then he started to walk around me, his eyes moving up and down and scrutinizing every part of me. Even though I was also naked, now I felt even more exposed than ever before.

And, glancing down at the place between his legs, I noticed his bulge and… Wow. It was massive. It was plump and massive, and the only thing I wanted to do right now was to start to massage it with my hands. But I wasn't even going to bring that up until he said it himself.

He stopped until he was in front of me again and then he thrust me against a wall after placing his hands on my shoulders. His lips were now mere moments from kissing me.

"You are mine, just like my wife is."

CHAPTER 3

Wait, that was his wife? I asked myself, realizing that I already knew the answer and thus there was no point in asking that question to him.

His lips were on the verge of kissing mine, and I had no idea if he was going to go through with it.

"I'm not going to do this. There's actually something that I want to do first," he announced before grabbing my hand and then taking me so that I was a little closer to the middle of the room while keeping his wife in my line of sight.

"Her name is Helene, by the way," he said as if he could read my mind. I had been asking myself what his wife's name was. I glanced at her, but she didn't want to look at me. She was still with her head lowered, looking down at the floor.

I had just about enough time to understand what was going on before it was too late. Geoffrey chained my arms and my legs, making my body form an X position. My legs now had a gap, which he could get under with very little effort. My pussy was now more exposed than it had ever been.

And Geoffrey did then get under me. He was supporting his weight with his hand and his knees, his eyes scanning my pussy. He smacked his lips, running his tongue from one side to the other.

"I can tell that you're a virgin, just from what I'm seeing," he murmured, running his finger on my pussy. I arched my back after feeling a wave of pleasure that he generated in me.

He smiled, saying, "you really like that, don't you? There are so many things that I'm going to do with you, so… manage your expectations, I suppose."

And just when I was wondering what he was going to do next, he grabbed both my legs, pulled himself up, and then stopped when his face was on the verge of being buried into my cunt.

He put his tongue out, licking and savoring my snatch, making sure that he was hitting all the right spots, and he was. I felt my body becoming like pudding, all the strength in it fading away. His fingers on my legs dug deeper into my skin, shooting pain in me that I welcomed.

Looking down, I could see how hard he was. It was such a pity that he hadn't taken off his clothes yet.

His tongue continued to lap and rub on my pussy lips, making me feel more pleasure than ever before in my life. I moaned and groaned, wishing that I was doing more. I wished that my hand was free so that I could start to rub my clit.

And then, as if Geoffrey was reading my mind, he did just that, scratching my clit with his finger. He was doing it so well that I knew it was going to happen. I was going to hit my climax, and it was going to be the most powerful one that I ever had in my life.

All of this still wasn't enough, though, I realized when Geoffrey stopped what he was doing. I looked down and found his eyes, showing that I was questioning him about what he wanted to do right now.

He propelled himself up, sliding his hands over my curves. His eyes showed me how much he wanted the only thing that he was thinking about at the moment. It was my milk. That was what he craved the most in this instance.

I could feel the heat of his body. I could feel his skin pressing against my body through his office suit, and also how hard and firm his muscles were.

And when I was going to open my mouth and I thought that he was going to start to fumble with my breasts, Geoffrey decided to do something else. He walked over to one of the other sides of the basement. It was so dark in there that I lost sight of him the moment he stepped into the darkness.

I heard something metallic and slightly plastic when he was in there. Then, I heard some rustling noise, and my mind started to imagine that he was taking off his clothes.

Seconds later, he didn't disappoint me. He came out from the darkness naked. From top to bottom, his body was nothing short of perfect, and when he was a couple more feet closer to me, his wife lifted her head again. Helene was looking at him, licking her lips.

It was at that moment when I realized, again, that she'd always wanted to be put into this humiliating position, chained to the wall like that, her body hurt. I doubted that she could even walk even if she weren't chained to the wall.

Geoffrey was holding something in his right hand. It was a ball gag, I realized the moment when he came a little bit closer to me.

"As it is in your contract, I can do everything and anything I want to you, dear," he said before positioning himself behind me and then fastening the ball gag on my head. He put it into my mouth, and I hated that he was doing this. When he finally penetrated me for the first time, I wanted to scream at the top of my lungs, but now that this ball gag was in my mouth, I was going to be unable to do that.

I felt his fingers on my shoulders, feeling them.

Then, I felt his nose sniffing my neck, his lips kissing the nape. "And I have to say, everything about you is so tempting. It's difficult not to skip all the foreplay and get to the best part," he murmured into my ear.

And then, I also felt his cock pressing against my butt, and then he moved away from me, picking up something that was behind me. I heard a noise in the basement. I knew what that was, and I was already waiting for the punishment that he was going to inflict on me with it.

My nipples were already leaking milk thinking about what was going to happen next.

CHAPTER 4

Geoffrey wasn't kidding when he said that this next part was going to be painful. I looked over my shoulder, finding out that he was holding a whip in his hand. A fucking whip! I couldn't believe what my eyes were witnessing, and yet it was so fucking tempting that I was licking my lips again.

"I'm going to milk your succulent jugs soon, dear," he announced, striking my back with the whip and making me feel a sharp pain that cut through my body.

Oh, fuck. That was almost too much.

"She's enjoying that, Master. Aren't you going to bring over your other bitch so that she can watch all of this happen, too?" Helene asked, making me wonder who she meant by 'that other bitch.'

But I soon realized that the answer to that was obvious. Geoffrey did indeed have someone else. Another woman. The first hucow he bought.

"I'll bring her here in a little bit," he replied, striking my back with the whip one more time. Pain shot through me, making my nipples hard. Milk oozed from them, wetting my skin.

Geoffrey was hard, more so than he'd been all day, I thought. I just couldn't wait until he was finally sinking that thick, meaty thing inside of me. That was all that was going on in my mind at the moment.

"How disappointing. Or maybe I should be saying that I'm lucky that this is happening like this. I mean, at least I don't have to share this moment with her again, like so many things that we have to share," Helene murmured, most likely wishing that her hand was free so that she could pleasure herself.

Geoffrey didn't hold anything back, striking my back one, two, three times, and then going on from there as if this was the first and last time we were seeing each other. It wasn't just the pain shooting through my body that was making me love everything going on here, of course, but also the blood coming out of the wounds.

By the time Geoffrey was done, my body was limp. The only thing preventing me from falling was the chains. They kept me almost suspended in the air.

Geoffrey dropped the whip, walking until he stood in front of me. His right hand grabbed my left boob, putting the nipple into his mouth. It fitted nicely. He started to suckle on it and apply pressure, drinking some of my milk. I could see a line of milk leaking through the right side of his mouth.

"Oh, God, this is so delicious," he purred before suckling on my boob a little more, and when I thought that that was going to be enough, he decided to show me something else. He grabbed my other breast and then put my right nipple into his mouth, focusing on the way that his lips were applying pressure on the textured skin.

His lips were hot and wet. I felt the way that they were working on my nipple. But even that wasn't enough for someone of his caliber. His other hand continued to worship my skin, sliding on the corners of my body. Then, he brought it around me and looked for my ass, which he cupped in an instant.

"Your skin is so soft and warm," he murmured, digging his fingers into my skin, and then continued doing that for a little while longer than he should.

As the minutes went on, I wondered how much milk I still had left in my breast. Geoffrey then pulled his head back, looking into my eyes and after I looked down, I noticed that his lips were smeared with my milk. That was such a huge turn-on that the only thing I wanted him to do was to finish this in style.

Geoffrey brought his hand down, looking for my clit while he positioned himself behind me. He started to rub on it, his other fingers prying and pulling at my pussy lips. I started to moan and groan, and then my eyes rolled inside my head when he did what I was hoping he was going to do.

Geoffrey picked up the pace, scratching and grazing his finger on my clit for what felt like an eternity, all the while grinding and thrusting his body against mine, teasing me that he was going to finally plunge inside of me with his meaty member soon.

Everything he was doing was enough to bring me over the edge and then I finally came, my body shaking and trembling as he continued to thrust and pound his hips against my ass. My body was sweaty and I loved that. I loved everything about this moment and the way that it was like my skin was on fire.

He kissed the nape of my neck over and over when I finally climbed down from my high. I was panting. I looked over my shoulder so that I could find his eyes and I knew that, from the way that he was staring back, there were so many more things he was going to do to me.

I could also feel the pre-come oozing from the slit of his cockhead, making me wonder when he was finally going to give me a taste of it.

Geoffrey then didn't waste any time, positioning himself behind me when he picked up something else.

What did he have in his hand this time? It was an electric baton. He was going to perform some sort of 'shock therapy' on me and, thinking that, I could already feel more of my milk oozing from my teats.

Teats. That was the right term, I thought. Not nipples.

CHAPTER 5

Geoffrey was holding the electrical baton in his right hand, showing it to me. "You want me to touch this to your skin, don't you?" He asked me and the only thing I could do was nod, still feeling milk oozing from my nipples. It was obvious that Geoffrey was going to need to milk my udders again when he had the chance.

Finally, he took the ball gag out of my mouth and I could talk and scream again.

"Yes, Master. That's everything I want," I confessed and even though I couldn't see his face, I knew he was smiling. He took a few steps toward me and then he pressed the tip of the baton to my back, sending an electrical shock through my body. I felt it shaking and twitching and I really thought I was going to pass out, but I didn't.

"This is exactly the kind of reaction I was expecting from you, my pretty little thing," he murmured right behind me, his hand sliding on my shoulder. He must have set up the baton to full power. I could hear the way that it crackled.

"You can do everything to me, Master. Please punish me for being so naughty," I said, breathless, and he did exactly that, though this time he was a lot more ruthless. He didn't just connect the baton to my skin, but he also thrust it onto it, making my body kick itself forward, his wife chuckling in the distance. But she wasn't really that far, so that was my mind just imagining things. Or maybe this whole punishment section was taking a bigger toll on me than I'd thought.

"I can do so much more with you, but I can see that it's not enough for someone like you, is it?" He asked the moment when I reopened my eyes and I noticed that someone was coming into the basement. *Into his sex dungeon,* to be more precise, I thought when I noticed a crawling figure coming toward me from the stairs.

"Who is that?" I asked and I felt Master touching the baton to my body again, making it shake and tremble. In the meantime, I was wondering when he would finally touch it in my pussy. I knew that when he did that, I would have another orgasm, and it would be mouthwatering.

"This is Jenna, my other hucow," he replied.

She almost looked hesitant to come forward, but then she came toward us, crawling. I could see the way that her boobs swayed as she moved, her body looking so big it was no wonder that she was crawling. She also had a collar around her neck, was naked, and had a mark on her skin, almost like she had been branded.

When she was closer to me, I could make out what that mark said. It had the initials for Geoffrey's full name. Geoffrey Lawrence. It must have hurt a lot, right? Geoffrey wasn't satisfied with what he had already done to me, so he decided to position himself by my side and then he pressed the baton to my cunt, shooting another electrical shock through my body. This time, he decided to keep it in contact with my clit, and this just went on and on, my body shaking, lips trembling, and I really thought that this time I was going to pass out and would never wake up.

Minutes later, I realized that I was still here. My body was like pudding and my heart was racing with the speed of a bullet train, but it was okay, and I just realized that Jenna wasn't smiling at me devilishly. I almost thought that she looked frightening, but the feeling that she was showing on her face was different from that. She was actually extremely turned on by the sight of me being punished for being naughty – or just for an introduction to living under Geoffrey's rule, to be honest.

"Jenna, you really like what you're seeing, right?" Master

asked, stepping around me. The baton was so close to touching my body that, while he continued to walk around me, the only thing I could keep on thinking about was when he would electrocute me with it again.

Jenna nodded. "Master, all I want right now is for you to punish her until she is begging for mercy," she said and I knew from then on that we would never be friends. She saw me as a competitor, as she should. After all, I wasn't going to leave this house and I was always going to strive to be my Master's favorite plaything.

"As you wish, Jenna. I doubt that she is going to survive this," Master announced, and I couldn't help but feel that what he just said was like a statement that was going to reflect the truth in the future. Still, I didn't think hard about it. I didn't care about it because the next thing he did was to press the electrical baton to my teats, sending more electrical shock through my entire body, and this time it was enough to make me come. It was so wild that milk started to ooze in copious amounts out of my teats, pooling on the floor of the basement. It was made of bricks, so all the milk filled the gaps between them.

It was a beautiful sight; I wasn't going to lie.

"That was incredible, Master," Jenna said, crawling over to me. I raised my eyebrow as I asked her what she was going to do, and then she showed me exactly what her plan was. She put her tongue out of her mouth and then started to lap up at my pussy and clit, creating more waves of pleasure in my helpless body.

And perhaps this was thanks to the fact that she was a woman, but the way she was licking and exciting my clit was marvelous, and I came one more time, and this time it was breathtaking, and I passed out.

In the meantime, just before darkness encroached my vision, the last thing I thought was when Master would finally take my virginity.

He had to, right?

CHAPTER 6

At least, that was what I was hoping for from Geoffrey. It was another day after that amazing first day here with him, and this time I wasn't in his sex dungeon. I was actually somewhere else. I was in his bedroom, where the bed looked messy. The pillows were in random positions on the mattress and the bedsheets were pulled to the top right side, exposing what was underneath.

Not even the bedroom itself was clean. There was this odor in the air, like someone had just had sex in here not too long ago. And despite that being a turn-off to some people, for me, it was a turn-on, and I couldn't help but wonder how it had been, Master fucking his wife and maybe Jenna, too.

Maybe? Of course that he fucked her too, I thought, feeling a rush of air entering the room when I noticed that he was here with me. Damn, he was fast, not to mention that it looked like he could go in and out of places unnoticed.

"Come on, pretty little thing. Lie down on the bed. Today, Daddy is going to take your virginity." He leaned, his lips close to nipping at my earlobe, but he didn't. Again, he was such a tease that it was maddening.

I lied down on the bed and I heard Geoffrey unscrewing something. He didn't need to use lube or anything of the sort, though. My cunt was dripping wet at this point, and it couldn't be any different.

He put down the bottle he was holding and then positioned himself on top of me. He was naked, I noticed. Just like on most other days, Geoffrey was naked. His hard, well-worked muscles pressed against my sensitive skin, making me even wetter than before. Then, he pulled himself up slightly, his lubed-up fingers oiling his thick, meaty dick.

Geoffrey ran his tongue through the gap of my ass and then he thrust inside of me, going all the way in one fell swoop. I thought that he was going to be a lot gentler about this, but that wasn't his style. He went inside of me all the way and only stopped when he felt that he couldn't go any deeper.

Oh, gosh. The pain. It was almost too much and I had to bite my lips really hard so that it didn't black out my vision. Then, Master started to thrust in and out of me, keeping his pace slow in the beginning. He huffed on top of me and his balls pressed against my ass, showing me again how deep he was.

Geoffrey also hit my g-spot every time and he was doing this so effortlessly, making sure that he was bringing me so much closer to my orgasm. In the meantime, I couldn't hide the smile that showed up on my face. He was taking my virginity. Or, to be more precise, he had already taken it and now he was just managing this until we reached the end.

He picked up the pace, pushing himself up so that he was sitting on the bed with his knees. I felt his hands pulling me up so that my ass was in constant contact with his pelvis. He bent his body over mine so that his abs and his chest were touching my back, and then, exhaling when his head was right behind the nape of my neck, he started to thrust in and out of me, increasing the pace to something that he was more comfortable with, I thought. After all, someone of his caliber had a lot of experience, and he was showing that to me right at this moment.

"Oh God, oh God," I let out over and over again as I felt his balls slapping off my butt. Geoffrey didn't stop there. He increased his pace so that his pelvis was moving so fast it was like a blur, and I could hear the way that the bed was creaking. It was shaking so much I thought that it was going to crumble and we were both going to fall down to the floor. Still, we didn't, thankfully. I supposed that this bed had gone through so much worse than this. It was 'experienced' with all the rounds of sex where Geoffrey fucked his properties.

He stopped when his cock was already shaking, erupting, and spurting out his pre-come inside of me. Geoffrey jammed it all the way inside of me, most likely to make sure that nothing was going to come out when he pulled out. And even after his cock was already softening and he wasn't shooting out his come inside of me anymore, he still didn't pull out.

I wondered when he would.

A month later, he finally did that and I felt like I was missing a limb. I felt my pussy hole trying to close again, but it couldn't. It would never be the same. Even after Geoffrey pulled out, it was still gaping, still open, and I could feel now, more noticeable than ever before, the cold air in the room going inside.

I collapsed on the bed, turning around. Geoffrey positioned his head on his hand as he gazed at me. "You liked that, didn't you, bitch?" He asked me and even though he called me a bitch, it didn't stop me from nodding and giving him the answer he expected from me.

To be honest, I was now only wondering what was going to happen in the coming months. Was he thinking about making another acquisition?

Another hucow?

EPILOGUE

It was another day. I was outside the house, holding a flower in my hands. I was naked and everyone could see me. Even the guards could see me naked, and I wanted them to see me like this. I wanted that because I wanted them to think about me going up and down on their cocks, something that could happen in the future.

It was beautiful outside. The sun was bright and warm, the clouds were white and fluffy-looking, and the sky itself was tinted with a shade of cyan. The wind swirled around me shyly, kissing my body.

I was sitting on the steps in front of the main door when my eyes caught sight of a car driving over to the front of the house. I wondered who that was. The car was a sedan and black, the sunlight shining off the frame.

The car pulled over and the driver stepped out, going around the vehicle to open the passenger door at the back. A leg stepped out of the car and then the rest of the body came out. It was a woman, I thought the moment when my eyes saw the curves of her body. She was wearing a trendy pair of sunglasses, shining under the sunlight.

She wore a dark red dress, high-heel sandals, and a long necklace on her neck. She turned her head around slowly, analyzing what was in the vicinity. Treading her fingers through her hair, it took her no more than a couple of seconds to notice me, and when she did, she curled up the right corner of her lips, showing me that she didn't like my presence here at all.

Who was she?

Just when I was going to start to think about all the possible answers to that question, I heard footsteps behind me. I looked up and found Geoffrey. Differently from most days when he was in his house, this time he wasn't naked.

He'd put on a French blue office suit, his hands in his pockets. A huge smile was plastered on his face. And that look in his eyes... Even though I didn't want to admit it, it was obvious it showed me that he had been waiting for this moment. He had been waiting for her arrival, and that realization alone was enough to stir jealousy in me.

Whoever that woman was, I already hated her.

The End

Thank you for reading this story. Leave your review. Your feedback helps me immensely!

TEASER: I'M HIS PROPERTY

Dark Hucow BDSM (Auction Club - 1)

He took my hand. His grip was strong. I felt his fingers around mine, and I couldn't do anything. I couldn't do anything because I was naked and also because I could feel his eyes boring into me, making me feel more uncomfortable than I already was.

"It's so nice that you have come here," he said. His name was Mr. Lawrence. For the time being, that was his name to me. The only name that I could use and that I could think of whenever I thought about him.

He was imperious. He was so much taller than me that I could wrap my arms around him and they would go under his armpits. He could rest his chin on top of my head, and he would be able to do that without going on his tiptoes.

He could make me feel so small with his body, which was something I never thought I would be feeling now that I was a hucow. I had gone through the transformation, and now here I was, about to be sold to him.

"Yeah, we had to come. We want to sell her and you said on the website that you were interested," my associate said. His name was Jake and he was here to sell me to Mr. Lawrence. He was a good guy and I was certain that he was going to do his best for the sales pitch, no doubt about it.

Mr. Lawrence eyed me up and down, his eyes scanning my body.

They rested on my boobs. That was what he wanted to see, wasn't it? The thing that he was waiting for the most. I was certain that was the case, and it was a reason for me to be proud of myself.

I had worked so hard to make my boobs as big as they could be, and it worked. My boobs were so big now that his hands would feel small when he started to play with them, I thought, hiding the smile that wanted to creep up on my face.

"Yeah, I said that. She really is something else, isn't she?" He asked, his eyes still lingering on my boobs. It felt like they would never stop staring at them, and that just might turn out to be the case, I thought, squirming my legs together.

My associate put his hand on my shoulder, stroking it. "We did everything possible to make it so she really fits your needs," he said, smiling devilishly. He had all the reasons to be smiling like that, even though we knew that nothing would happen between us.

He had always said he felt something for me, but I was certain that it was nothing more than just a hucow-associate crush, and it would never lead to anything.

"I can see that you did. Her breasts are so big, so perky, and they look heavy, too," Mr. Lawrence said, and I could tell that the only thing he wanted to do right now was to be with his hands all over me.

In the meantime, I couldn't help but look down, seeing his cock under his pants. He wasn't doing anything to hide his erection, and that wasn't surprising. He knew he was on top of everything and that I was going to do everything he wanted, even though there was going to be a safe word that we were going to decide on later.

"We really outdid ourselves when transforming her," Jake said, his hand moving down and making me wonder if he was going to do what I was thinking he was. Cupping my ass. His hand was close, but it wasn't quite there yet, I thought.

"Yeah, you really did," Mr. Lawrence said, stepping to the side and holding out his hand. He was inviting us inside his house. "Please, come in. Let's sit down and have something to drink."

His house? I thought, realizing how stupid I was. It was more like a mansion. It was big. It was impressive. It was fit for a billionaire, and I couldn't help but feel I was out of place here. I pretty much was, I thought.

I would never live in a place quite like this, and that was a given.

Either way, this was going to be my new house. Just on the far side, I noticed a portrait hanging above the fireplace. It showed Mr. Lawrence and Mrs. Lawrence, his wife.

I didn't know her, and I actually also didn't know much about Mr. Lawrence, either. He was walking in front of us, leading us inside the house. We were in the main hall, and from here we could reach the second floor of the house. I felt so small in this place, and I knew it would take me a lot of time to get used to it.

"Whoa," I said, looking around and almost tripping and losing my balance. Thankfully, that didn't happen. Had that happened, I would be so flustered and looking so confused I would never know where to bury my head.

"This is all mine," Mr. Lawrence said as if it needed to be said. Of course it was all his.

We reached what appeared to be the living room in the house. He sat down, ordered one of the waiters to bring us something to drink, and I couldn't focus on anything that he said. Either way, I knew that it was going to be something nice. Something to break the ice between us.

He sat down with his legs spread apart, his erection still showing under his pants.

As if to show me that this was his dominion, his territory, he held nothing back before putting his fingers under his pants, starting to stroke his hardness. Wow.

I didn't think he was just going to start doing that, and it was hot. It was a turn-on, and I suddenly found myself even more flustered than before. I knew that he could see the red tint on my cheeks.

And he was smiling devilishly without showing his teeth.

SIMILAR BOOKS

BUNDLE - HUCOW PRISON

All the books of the Hucow Prison series in one single, convenient collection.

1. Hucow Prison

SERIES - BUMPED HUCOWS

1. Milked by Rockstars

2. Tamed by Rockstars

3. Taken by Rockstars

4. Claimed by Rockstars

SERIES - HIS HERD

1. Peculiar Dairy

2. Milked by her Boyfriend

3. Menage for Milking

4. Farm Milking

5. Fertile for my Farmers

ABOUT THE AUTHOR

Leandra Camilli's obsession? Writing dirty, steamy stories that make her readers drool. She loves her Alpha males, hucows, sissies, and futas. If you're looking for those kinds of books, look no further.

With a cup of coffee on her table and warm socks on, she writes almost every day. Leandra Camilli has featured in several top 100 categories in the store, and she publishes weekly.